# THE TORTILLA QUILT

### Story ◆ Recipe ◆ Quilt Pattern

THE TORTILLA QUILT
COPYRIGHT © 1996 JANE TENORIO-COSCARELLI

PUBLISHER: JANE TENORIO-COSCARELLI
COPY EDITORS: CONNIE CUTLER, MARK KOSCIELAK
TECHNICAL EDITOR: JANET NEEPER

QUILT DESIGNER AND MAKER: LINDA SAWREY
QUILTED BY: ARNETTE JASPERSON
FABRIC SUPPLIED BY: P& B TEXTILES

QUILT PHOTOGRAPHY BY: CARINA WOOLRICH PHOTOGRAPHY
ARTIST PORTRAIT BY: SANDRA . DAVID FINE PHOTOGRAPHY

PUBLISHED BY
1/4 INCH PUBLISHING
39165 SILKTREE DRIVE
MURRIETA, CA. 92563  USA

LIBRARY OF CONGRESS CATALOG  CARD NUMBER: 96-92477

ISBN HB: 0-9653422-0-4
ISBN PB: 0-9653422-1-2

PRINTED IN HONG KONG
BY REGENT  PUBLISHING SERVICES

10 9 8 7 6 5 4

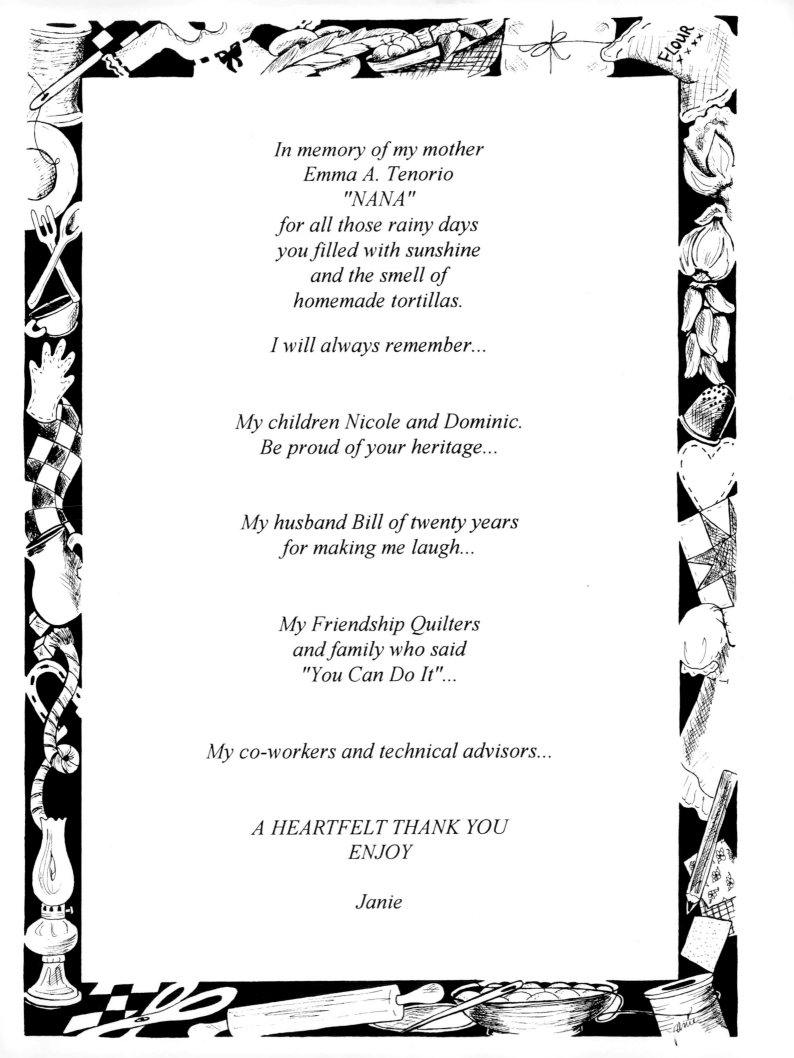

*In memory of my mother*
*Emma A. Tenorio*
*"NANA"*
*for all those rainy days*
*you filled with sunshine*
*and the smell of*
*homemade tortillas.*

*I will always remember...*

*My children Nicole and Dominic.*
*Be proud of your heritage...*

*My husband Bill of twenty years*
*for making me laugh...*

*My Friendship Quilters*
*and family who said*
*"You Can Do It"...*

*My co-workers and technical advisors...*

*A HEARTFELT THANK YOU*
*ENJOY*

*Janie*

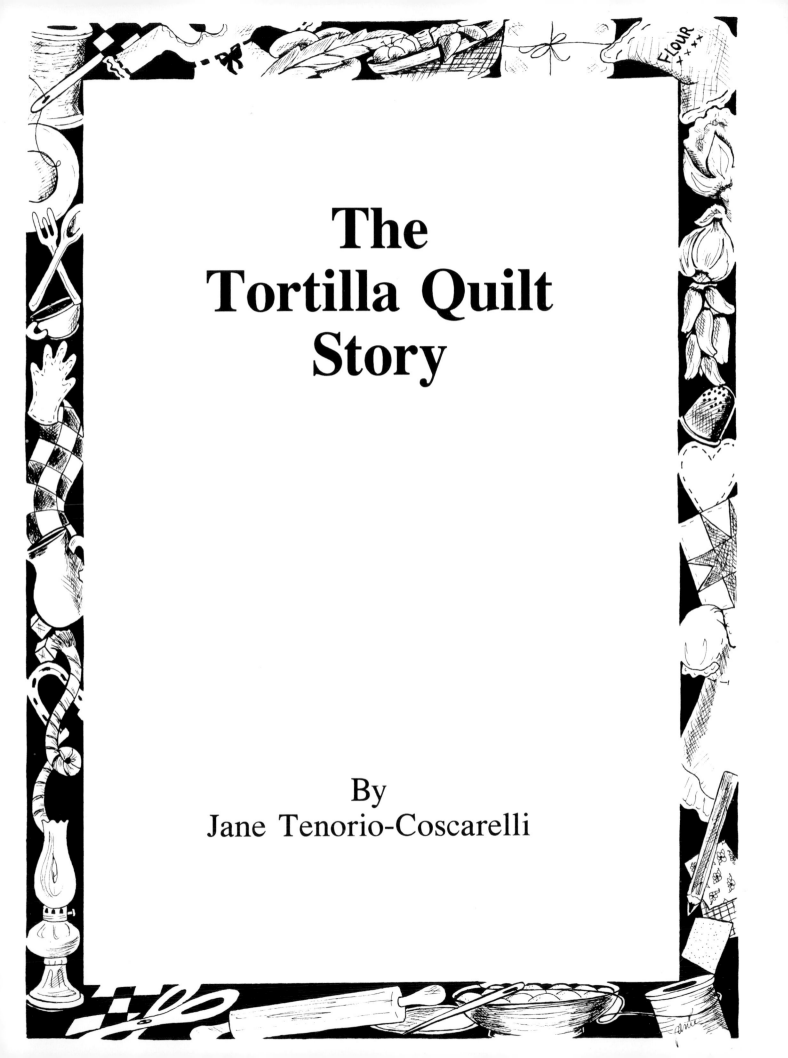

# The
# Tortilla Quilt
# Story

## By
## Jane Tenorio-Coscarelli

Maria lived with her grandmother Lupita
*abuela*
on a large ranch in California.  Lupita worked
*rancho grande*
as a cook for the Olson family.  Maria would
*familia*
help her grandmother daily.  She would rise

early in the morning to start her chores before
*mañana*
the rest of the family was up.

Maria would tend the chickens daily and

go out to the chicken coop to gather eggs to
*pollera* *huevos*
prepare breakfast for the Olson family.
*desayuno*
Grandmother Lupita would be busy making

tortillas.

Maria's best friend was Sarah Olson.  She
*amiga*
was lucky to live with someone her own age.

The ranch was large and had many horses and
*caballos*
donkeys.  Sarah and Maria would ride and
*burros*
play together all day.

5

After the evening meal, Maria would

watch Sarah sit and sew by lamp light with
*sentarse*                 *luz*
her mother.  They were making a quilt
*madre*
together.  They would talk and laugh together.

Maria wanted so much to make a quilt too.

She would tell her grandmother about the

beautiful quilts Sarah and her mother were
*bellas*
making, but she knew she did not have all the

pretty colored fabric like Sarah.  A quilt
*bonita*          *tela*
would be so expensive for her to make.

Lupita could see the disappointment on

Maria's face.
*cara*

One day, while making tortillas for the

morning meal, Maria's grandmother realized

she had a dozen flour and meal sacks in the
*docena*
pantry.  She thought the sacks might work for

Maria's quilt.

She called Maria into the kitchen and sat
*cocina*
her at the table.   Grandmother Lupita gave
*mesa*
Maria a square template of kindling wood to
*leña*
use as a pattern.   Maria traced and cut the
*cortó*
square pieces out very carefully with scissors.

She would place them neatly on the table.

She was so excited about her quilt she had

to share it with her best friend Sarah.  Sarah

saw the quilt of flour sacks and how hard

Maria was working on cutting the fabric.

Sarah told Maria she needed a little color in
                                        *color*
her quilt.  So Sarah went to her mother for
                                        *madre*
help.

15

Mrs. Olson said she had some of Maria

and Sarah's dresses that they had outgrown.
*vestidos*
Sarah and Maria could cut them up for quilt

squares.  The quilt began to grow and grow.

It now took up the whole table.

Soon Maria had to set it on the

kitchen floor.  Sarah and Maria would spend
*suelo de la cocina*
hours playing with all the pieces, deciding

where each needed to be.  Like a jigsaw

puzzle of fabric and memories, the pieces

began to fit together.  Maria's birthday dress,
*cumpleaños*
Sarah's Christmas dress, a blouse with little
*Navidad*
flowers that was Maria's favorite.  Each
*flores*
fabric square saying, remember me.

19

Soon the girls decided it was time to sew

the pieces together. Sarah brought out her

sewing basket. She gave Maria a needle,
*canasta*
thread, and a thimble. Maria tried to put the
*hilo*        *dedal*
thimble on her thumb. This made Sarah

laugh. She told Maria to put it on her other

finger. The thimble would help push the

needle through the fabric.

They sat by the fire and tenderly stitched
*fuego*
each piece together.  Maria's grandmother

was so very proud of how hard the girls
*orgullosa*
worked together on the quilt top.

When they finished the top of the quilt,

Lupita put the black iron on the woodburning
*plancha negra*
stove.  When it was hot enough, she pressed
*estufa*                    *caliente*
the top nice and flat.

Then Sarah said they needed batting for

the quilt.  She asked her mother if she could

help with Maria's quilt.  Mrs. Olson went to

her sewing room and returned with some
*cuarto*

pieces of cotton batting.  The girls could see
*pedazos*

some seeds in the cotton fabric.  It would
*semillas*          *algodón*

make the quilt good and warm.

They happily stitched the pieces together.

For the backing of the quilt they stitched

together the rest of the flour sacks.  You

*harina*

could see labels of all the different flour and

meal companies on the back of the quilt.

Lupita again heated the iron and pressed the

back nice and flat.

29

She then laid it on the kitchen floor.  Then
*puso*                                    *suelo*
they laid the batting over the backing.  Lastly,

they laid the pieced quilt on top.  Sarah and

Maria took big basting stitches to hold the

quilt together so it would not move or slip

apart.

Mrs. Olson said Maria could use her big wooden quilting frame. This was a special honor for Maria's quilt, because it would

*honor*

remain in the Olson family parlor until they finished quilting the quilt.

For many evenings the women of the
        *noches*      *mujeres*
house---Maria, Sarah, Mrs. Olson, and even

Grandma Lupita---quilted on the quilt.  Maria

quilted hearts in the squares because she loved
    *corazones*
her quilt so.  Sarah quilted feathers in the
                        *plumas*
borders because it reminded her of the ranch

chickens and how she and Maria would steal

their eggs.  Mrs. Olson quilted hands because
                  *manos*
so many hands had worked on the quilt.

Lupita quilted angel wings because the girls
          *alas*
were her little angels.  They stitched and

laughed and told stories of the ranch.  When
        *cuentos*
they were done, Mrs. Olson showed Maria

how to bind the edge of her quilt.

35

When Maria finished the last stitches on

her quilt, the girls laid it on Sarah's white

iron bed. They picked out the colors of the
*cama*                                    *colores*
dresses they wore when they were little and

told stories of each different fabric.  Sarah

asked Maria what she was going to do with

the quilt.

Maria wrapped it in paper and said,
*papel*
"follow me."  Sarah followed her into the

kitchen.  Maria's grandmother had just

finished making tortillas and was cleaning up.

Maria asked her to sit down for a
*sentarse*
minute.  The girls stood next to each other

giggling.  Maria hid the package behind her

back.  Lupita asked what they were up to.

Maria handed her grandmother the package.
*paquete*
She asked what it was.  "It's not my

birthday!"
*cumpleaños*
Maria said, "Go ahead, grandmother, open

it."

The girls watched as she unwrapped the

package.  There was the quilt with all its
*paquete*
colors and fine quilting stitches.  Maria told

her grandmother to read the back of the quilt.

In the corner, in Maria's finest embroidery
*mejor*
was stitched:


*The Tortilla Quilt for Grandmother Lupita*
*From Her Angels*
*Maria and Sarah*
*1880*

Maria's grandmother wrapped the quilt

around them both.  With a tear in her eye, she
                              *lágrima*          *ojo*
hugged and kissed each on the forehead.  She
              *besó*
said the tortilla quilt would keep her warm on

cold nights with memories of them both
*noches frías*
growing up.

Maria now has the tortilla quilt and tells

her own daughter the stories of her childhood
*hija*
on the ranch and of how the tortilla quilt came

to be one day in her grandmother Lupita's
*abuela*
kitchen so many quilts ago.  She reminds her

daughter that quilts not only warm the body,

but they also warm the heart.  At this, she
*corazón*
remembered the tortilla quilt and smiled.
*sonrió*

## THE END

47

# GRANDMA LUPITA'S FLOUR TORTILLAS
## TORTILLAS DE HARINA

4 cups flour                6 tablespoons shortening or oil
2 teaspoons salt            1 to 1¼ cups lukewarm water

Sift dry ingredients, add shortening, working it into the flour. Stir in 1 cup water and form into a ball; more water can be added if necessary, until bowl is clean of all dough. Knead well on floured board and make balls the size of an egg. Let them stand for 15 minutes; then roll out with rolling pin until they are salad plate size. Place on hot ungreased skillet or griddle on top of stove, cook for about 2 minutes on one side, then turn to other side and cook 1 minute longer. Serve freshly made or reheat later.

# THE TORTILLA QUILT

**"46 X 52"**
**Designer: Linda Sawrey**

# THE TORTILLA QUILT - INSTRUCTIONS
## "46 x 54"
### (Block Size 6" finished)

**FABRIC REQUIREMENTS-** 1/4 yd. of 11 different fabrics. This will give you extra, but for variety you will need that many fabrics.

**FIRST BORDER-** 1/4 yd. of fabric

**SECOND BORDER-** 3/4 yd. - if using a stripe as pictured, you will need 1 3/4 yd.

**BACKING-** 2 1/2 yd. (or piece leftover scraps of fabric)

**BINDING-** 1/2 yd. of fabric

From each fabric cut: (all measurements include 1/4" seam allowance)

       1 - 3 1/2" square (A)
       4 - 2 x 3 1/2 rectangle (B)
       4 - 2" squares (C)
       2 - 6 1/2 squares (alternate blocks)

**PIECING:** note all piecing uses 1/4" seam allowance.

Choose two fabrics and combine as shown below in block piecing diagram.

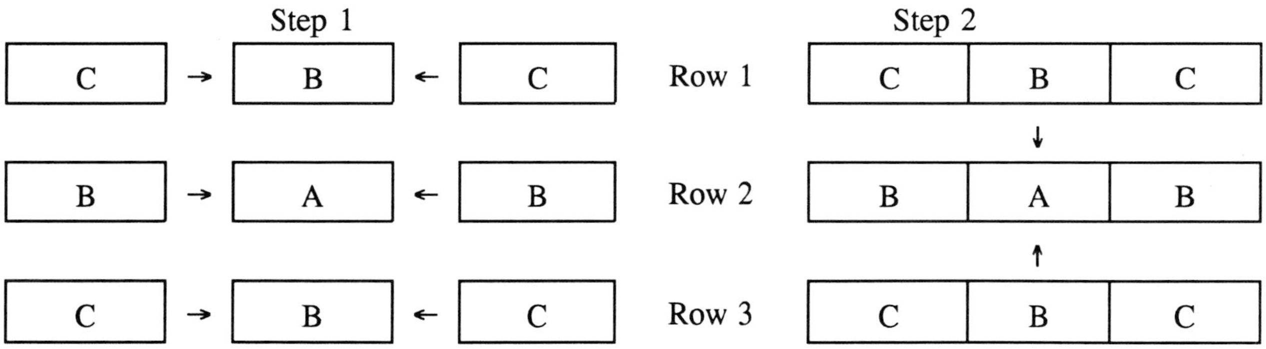

| Step 1 | | | | Step 2 | | |
|---|---|---|---|---|---|---|
| C → | B ← | C | Row 1 | C | B | C |
| | | | | | ↓ | |
| B → | A ← | B | Row 2 | B | A | B |
| | | | | | ↑ | |
| C → | B ← | C | Row 3 | C | B | C |

After each unit is sewn together, sew Row 1, 2, and 3 together.
Make 21 blocks. Alternate blocks with 6 1/2 solid squares refering to photo.
This quilt is 6 blocks across and 7 blocks down.

**FIRST BORDER-** Cut 1 1/2" strips and sew to top and bottom of center. Then sew strips to sides. Square up corners. Press.

**SECOND BORDER-** Cut 4 1/2" strips and add to quilt as in first border. Press.

**BASTE-** Lay flat - backing, batting, and quilt top. Baste to hold in place.

**QUILTING-** Quilt is quilted in the ditch around each block. Quilt patterns are in each solid block.

**BINDING-** Cut 5 - 2 1/2" strips. Sew together end to end. Fold in half wrong sides together. Press. Sew to top of quilt, raw edges out. Press, turn, and tack to back of quilt. Refer to basic quilting book for instructions. Press. Add label to back of quilt.

# Quilting Patterns

**Heart**

**Feather**

# Quilting Patterns

Hand

Angelwings

Other Products Available
From 1/4 Inch Designs:

Patterns:
  Summer Picnic
  Heart of My Heart
  Fall Friends
  Seasonal Folkland
  Spring Seeds
  Funkins
  Winter Willie
  Bunny Hop
  Material Garden
  Teas the Season
  Tea 4 II
  Baby Makes III
  Coffee Girls
  Remote Possibilities

Pins:
  Mummie Mia
  Mr. Kitty
  Friendship Heart Pin

Misc.:
  Quiltabeast Mugs
  Quiltabeast Tote Bags
  Quiltabeast T-Shirts

**1/4 Inch Publishing Co.**
**39165 Silktree Drive**
**Murrieta, CA  92563**
**(909) 677-5915**
*Patterns* ◆ *Book* ◆ *Notions*